Story and pictures by **James Proimos**

Scholastic Press • New York

Library of Congress Cataloging-in-Publication Data

Proimos, James, author, illustrator.
Waddle! Waddle! / by James Proimos.   pages   cm
Summary: A penguin waddles along, searching for the dancing friend he met yesterday,
while encountering other penguins and a hungry seal on the way.
ISBN 978-0-545-41846-1
1. Penguins—Juvenile fiction. 2. Friendship—Juvenile fiction. [1. Penguins—Fiction. 2. Friendship—Fiction.]
I. Title. PZ7.P9432Wad 2015   [E]—dc23   2014042778

10 9 8 7 6 5 4 3 2 1   15 16 17 18 19

Printed in Malaysia   108
First edition, December 2015

The display and text type was hand-lettered, and set in Boopee Regular.
Book design by Marijka Kostiw

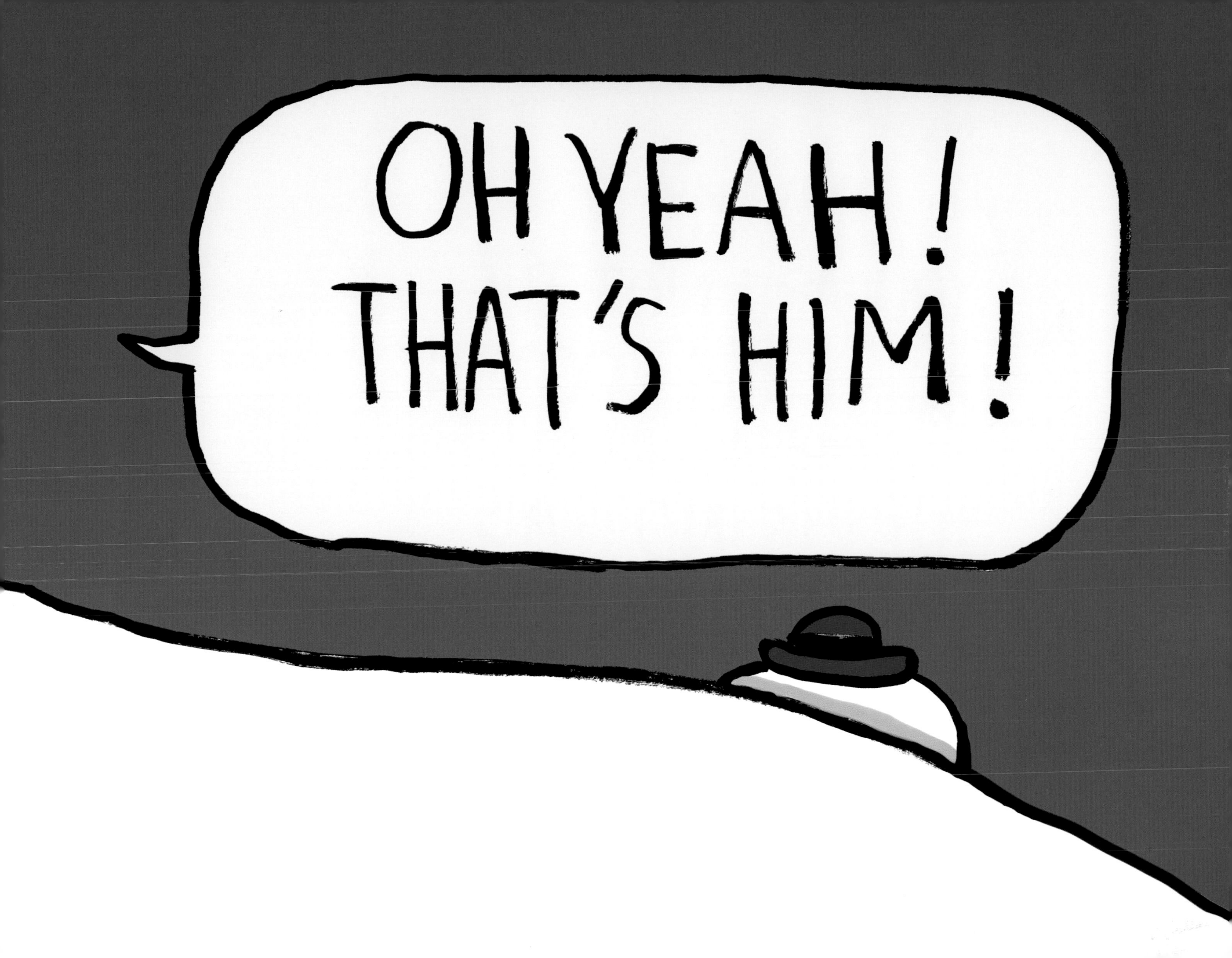
OH YEAH! THAT'S HIM!

MY, MY. YOU ARE NOT THE ONE I AM LOOKING FOR AT ALL. HE IS NOT AS TALL AS YOU.

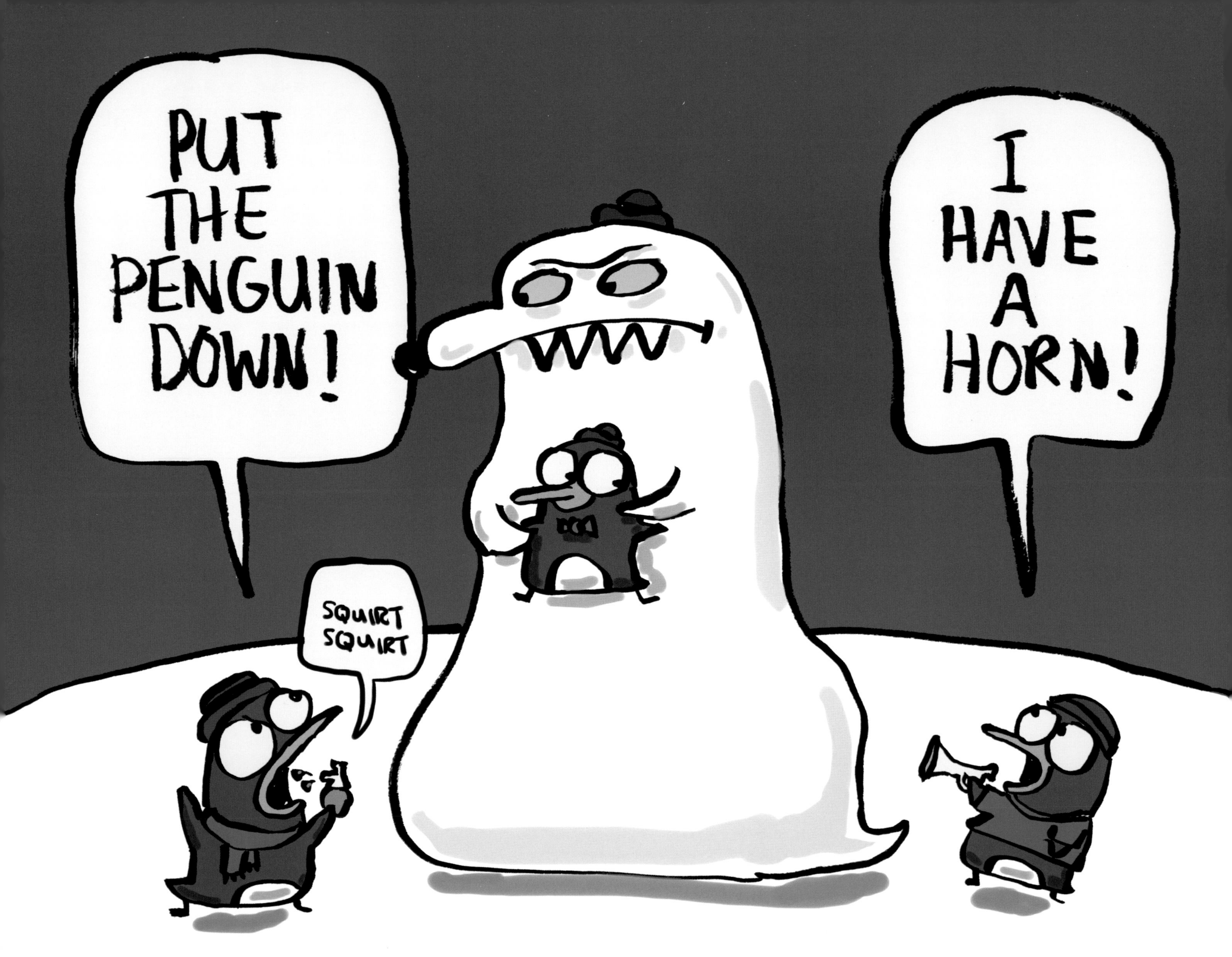
PUT THE PENGUIN DOWN!
I HAVE A HORN!
SQUIRT SQUIRT